A FILM BY TIM BURTON

A FILM BY TIM BURTON

Disney

FRANKENWEENIE

ADAPTED BY
ELIZABETH RUDNICK

BASED ON THE SCREENPLAY BY
JOHN AUGUST

BASED ON AN ORIGINAL IDEA BY
TIM BURTON

Disney PRESS

NEW YORK

A FILM BY TIM BURTON

Disney

FRANKENWEENIE

CHAPTER ONE

I t was a perfect day in the small and peaceful town of New Holland. The sun was shining and birds were chirping. Kids played hide-and-seek while parents drank lemonade on the porches of their cookie-cutter homes and gossiped about the latest happenings. On a hill above town, a Dutch windmill turned lazily in the soft wind. Everything was normal. Well, almost everything. Inside one particular house on Maple Lane, things were a little more . . . theatrical.

Mr. and Mrs. Frankenstein sat in their living room, waiting. Suddenly there was a whir followed by a hum and a moment later a projection screen flickered to life. A title card appeared on the screen. It was blurry and clearly homemade, but the title could just be made out. It read: MONSTERS FROM BEYOND!

Standing behind his twin homemade movie projectors ten-year old Victor Frankenstein observed his handiwork. Good. Everything was going just as he had planned. He fiddled with a button and was about to continue his show, when . . .

"Victor," a woman's voice said, sounding confused. "I don't know that it's . . ."

"You have to wear the glasses," Victor replied, running a hand through his thick dark hair. His mother didn't always understand him—or his inventions. He was used to it by now. But at least she supported him and his ideas.

"Oh! Yes, of course!" she said, reaching over to pick up the pair of 3-D glasses on the coffee table. Placing them on her face, her eyes grew wide. That was much, *much* better. The title card disappeared from view and was replaced by a new one. It read: STARRING SPARKY!

"That's you!" Mr. Frankenstein exclaimed. Victor's father looked like an older version of his son. He had dark hair and was tall, with long, lanky limbs. Looking at the screen and then down at a spot right next to him, he smiled. Sitting on the couch was Sparky the dog. The terrier was thirty pounds of wiggly body and wagging tail. His coat was white, and he had tall, pointy black ears that stood straight up. Hearing Mr. Frankenstein's shout, Sparky looked up and cocked his head. Victor's father reached down and gave the dog a pat before turning his attention back to the movie.

On the screen, Sparky had been transformed into the Sparkysaurus—a dog/dinosaur hybrid. He was wearing a foam fin on his back as he walked through a model city made completely of cardboard and household objects. An old refrigerator box was now a skyscraper and a candlestick acted as a lamppost. "So that's where my candlestick went," Mrs. Frankenstein said, as Sparky passed by the light.

"I've been looking for those golf tees," Mr. Frankenstein added, noticing a dozen or so of the pointy objects.

The Sparkysaurus suddenly came to a stop. Slowly, he turned around, his attention caught by something in the distance. As the camera panned out, the Frankensteins saw what the Sparkysaurus had seen—a pterodactyl. It was flying down from a mountain, right at the Sparkysaurus! Of course, in reality it was just a toy pterodactyl being held up by a fishing line, but its eyes glowed red with the help of old Christmas lights, so it still looked pretty scary. The Sparkysaurus didn't back down. Jumping up, Sparkysaurus grabbed the flying dinosaur in his mouth and began shaking his head back and forth. The pterodactyl didn't have a chance!

On the couch, the real Sparky got into the action. Jumping onto the back of the couch, he began to bark loudly at the screen. "You tell him, Sparky!" Mr. Frankenstein shouted, encouraging his furry little friend.

The light from the projector behind Sparky cast his shadow onto the screen, and for a moment it looked almost as if there were two Sparky's. But then the real Sparky moved a little and his silhouette disappeared.

Victor was pleased. Everything was going well. The movie looked good. His parents seemed entertained, and Sparky was perfect, as always. He was the best dog a boy could have. Nothing could ruin this moment. . . .

And then, everything went wrong.

Suddenly, one of the projectors began to hum and whir a bit too noisily. Something had caught on one of the splices in the film reel where Victor had pasted two sections of movie together. The projector jammed and then, as Victor watched in horror, the film caught on fire and began to melt. Meanwhile, one tail of the film came loose and began to whip back and forth just like Sparky's tail when he saw a squirrel. It went left and right, left and right, until it got tangled with the other projector's reel. With a SMASH, the machines got pulled together in a shower of sparks.

"Oh, my!" Victor's mom explained.

Woof, woof! Sparky barked.

Mr. Frankenstein was speechless.

Victor looked back and forth between the projectors, his mind racing. He had to do something. With a sigh he reached down and pulled the power cord from the wall. The light bulb on top of the projector dimmed, and the whirring reels slowed.

For a moment, the room went dark. Then Victor walked over and flicked on the light switch.

"It was certainly exciting!" Mrs. Frankenstein

said after a moment of awkward silence.

Her husband nodded. "Yeah! Big finish!"

Victor shook his head. He knew his parents were just being supportive. But he wasn't going to give up. "I can fix it," he said stubbornly. Picking up the remains of his projection machines, he patted his leg. "C'mon, boy!" he said, calling Sparky.

As Victor's parents watched him head upstairs with Sparky at his heels, they exchanged glances. It was nice that Victor was so inventive, but all these projects and crazy schemes were beginning to make them nervous.

"All that time he spends up there . . ." Mr. Frankenstein began, unsure if he should go on. He plunged ahead anyway. "A boy his age needs to be outside with his friends."

Mrs. Frankenstein shrugged. "I don't know that Victor has friends, dear," she answered.

"Other than Sparky."

"When I was his age, I had *lots* of friends. We'd play baseball until dark."

Victor's mom knew her husband was concerned. But when she had been a kid she had been a lot like Victor—quiet and shy. Mrs. Frankenstein had spent most of her time in her room, reading. And she had turned out fine. "There's nothing wrong with Victor," she said, ending the conversation. "He's just in his own world. . . ."

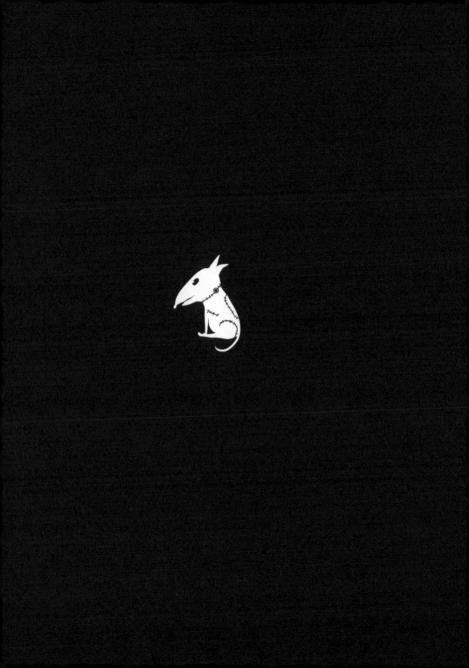

CHAPTER TWO

Upstairs, Victor was indeed in his own world. When he had begun making his inventions, his mom had let him keep them in his room. But soon there were just too many. So his parents had let him take over the attic and make it into his own private work space. He loved pulling down the trapdoor and walking up the ladderlike stairs into his invention wonderland. The ceiling was sloped on either side and there was a window that let in sunlight, moonlight, and the occasional bit of rain when Victor forgot to shut it. There was a workbench in the middle of the room covered with schematics, wires, and various tools. More schematics hung on the walls and every nook and cranny held fabulous inventions both new and old. It was Victor's haven.

After clearing off some space, he lifted his broken projectors onto the workbench. He needed to make some adjustments. Then everything would be in working order. As he disassembled the machine, Sparky jumped up onto his special Sparky-size treadmill. Victor had made it so his dog could get exercise even when Victor was too busy to walk him. As Sparky trotted along, Victor picked up a soldering iron. Putting on his safety glasses and pulling up his sleeves, he began tinkering.

While Victor tinkered, Sparky kept on trotting. He was used to his owner making lots of noise. He didn't mind. He just liked being near his boy. He kept on trotting as a plume of smoke rose out of Victor's soldering iron. Suddenly, he had an itch. Forgetting that the treadmill was still going, Sparky stopped to scratch himself. Whoosh! He went sliding backward, right off the treadmill. Victor heard the commotion and turned, but by the time he looked over, Sparky was back on the treadmill, his tail wagging.

Turning back to his projectors, Victor
narrowed his eyes. He fiddled with a lever and
patched up one last piece of film. Then he flashed
one of his rare smiles. He had fixed it! The day
wasn't going to end badly after all. Giving Sparky a
pat, Victor headed downstairs. He had homework
to do and dinner to eat. Tomorrow he could start
on a new invention.

The next morning, Victor waited on his front steps
for Sparky to grab the newspaper. It was one of
their rituals. Sparky would wait for the paperboy
to fling the news, run and grab it with his mouth,
and trot it right back to Victor. As Victor stood
waiting, he noticed that their next-door neighbor,
Mr. Burgemeister, was getting his own paper. Mr.
Burgemeister was not just Victor's neighbor. He
was also the mayor of New Holland—and a bit of
a bully. He spent hours making sure his flower

gardens looked just right, and if Sparky even looked at a tulip the wrong way, Victor was sure to hear about it.

As if he knew the boy was thinking about him, Mr. Burgemeister looked up and locked eyes with Victor. He sneered. "Your dog has been sniffing around my Dutch Dazzlers," he said nastily. "And the other day I caught him peeing on my flamingo."

"I'll keep an eye on him," Victor said, trying to sound sincere.

"You better," the mayor threatened. "Or I'll get you—and your little dog, too!" He let out a quick, evil laugh, proud of his clever quoting of the classic *Wizard of Oz.*

But what he didn't realize was that Victor didn't watch movies. He was too busy reading or inventing. So he had no idea what the man was talking about. He simply said, "Yes, sir," turned, and went inside, Sparky right behind him.

Mr. Burgemeister watched the Frankenstein's front door close. When he was convinced that the boy and his pesky dog wouldn't bother him, at least for the time being, he turned his attention back to the paper in his hand. Unfolding the front page, he scanned the headline. MAYOR BURGEMEISTER TO KICK OFF DUTCH DAY. Underneath was a picture of the mayor wearing a sash and hat. Mr. Burgemeister nodded, pleased.

Suddenly, sensing someone behind him, the mayor looked up from his paper. "And just where are you headed?" he asked the young girl with raven-dark hair sneaking out of the house.

It was his niece, Elsa Van Helsing. She was the same age as Victor and equally shy. Her hair was always pulled into two neat pigtails, and she always looked tidy. From her room, she had seen her uncle talking to Victor and hoped he'd be distracted long enough for her to sneak out. But she was out of luck.

At the sound of her uncle's voice, Elsa froze. She had been living with him long enough to know he had a short temper. "I'm going to school," she answered as politely as possible.

Mr. Burgemeister puffed out his chest. "Listen, your parents aren't back for another three months so . . ."

Elsa tried not to groan. Three months seemed like forever. She cut her uncle off before he could go on and listed her daily chores. "I made my bed. And my lunch. I cleaned up the kitchen and folded the towels."

When she was done, Mr. Burgemeister turned to face her. "Well, my darling niece," he said, his voice softening a touch. "I do appreciate your tidiness—unlike your parents, digging a bunch of holes in the desert."

CHAPTER TWO

"It's called archeology."

Mr. Burgemeister shrugged. "Whatever. It's pointless, really. And filthy. Everything worth anything is new, isn't it?" he said. "You don't go to a store and say, 'I'd like an old pot, please. And if you'd break it for me, that be even better.'" Satisfied his point had been made, he gestured to the road. "Off you go."

"Yes, sir," Elsa said, quickly walking down the path and away from the house. That conversation had been too long for her. Next time she'd have to hope Victor would distract her uncle a few minutes longer. Then she could get out without having to deal with that again. If only Victor weren't so shy. Then she could ask him to help her by inventing some way to make her invisible or something . . . if he would just talk to her.

CHAPTER THREE

Victor didn't know Elsa needed his help. He just knew he had to get to class on time. Everyday he took the same route to school. He rode his bike by Pine Street and Willow. Then he passed old Mrs. Reinhardt's creepy house, followed by a dozen picture perfect homes—each with big picture windows and two car garages.

Sometimes Sparky would sneak out of the house and follow until Victor made him turn around. Victor hated sending Sparky home. He wished he could take his dog with him to school. It would be so much nicer to have his best friend by his side. But he had tried that once. The principal had not been happy when he found Sparky inside Victor's locker. Now Sparky stayed tied up in the backyard or up in the attic, and Victor was all alone.

When he finally got to school, Victor kneeled down and locked his bike to a long rack. He was about to stand up when a shadow fell across him. Gulping, he raised his head.

Standing over him was the weirdest girl he'd ever met. She was even weirder than Victor, and that was saying a lot. She had huge eyes and long, stick-straight hair that made her skinny body seem even skinnier. Skulking around the school hallways, staring at the other students with her big eyes, she often looked as though she were plotting something. And to make matters worse, she had a big white cat named Mr. Whiskers that she believed could tell the future.

She was holding the cat as she stared down at Victor. Looking just like a villain out of a scary movie, she slowly stroked the cat's white fur. "Hello, Victor," the Weird Girl finally said.

"Hi," Victor replied.

"Mr. Whiskers had a dream about you last night," the girl said, holding the cat closer to her chest.

CHAPTER THREE

Victor sighed. If Sparky were there, he would have barked and scared off the cat and Victor wouldn't have to deal with this conversation. But Sparky was at home, so he had no choice but to ask, "How do you know?"

The girl gave one of her weird smiles. "Because this morning, he made this." She held out her arm and opened her palm. In her hand was something that looked like a small rope of dried clay. It was bent into the shape of a *V.*

Victor recoiled. "Did you get that out of the litter box?" he asked, disgusted.

The girl nodded. "It's an omen," she said, as though that were obvious. This wasn't the first time Mr. Whiskers had "made" an omen. It always happened the morning after he had one of his special dreams. "Last month he dreamed about Bob," the girl went on, referring to one of their classmates. Bob was a chubby guy who loved his food—especially ice cream. "That day he fell in a manhole."

When Victor didn't say anything, the girl gave another example. "He dreamed about Toshiaki the day he pitched a perfect game."

Victor remembered that day. It *had* been pretty impressive. Toshiaki was the foreign-exchange student in their class. He was an intense guy who loved baseball more than anything else—except winning. On the day Weird Girl was talking about, he *had* been even better than usual. Could it have been because of Mr. Whiskers?

"And he dreamed about Nassor the day he got knocked unconscious," the girl went on.

Victor remembered that, too. He didn't like Nassor. He was an intense boy with sinister eyes. During Toshiaki's perfect game, he had hit Nassor square on the mask, knocking him out.

While those were all pretty strange coincidences, Victor didn't necessarily believe that Mr. Whiskers had anything to do with them. But the girl clearly did. "If Mr. Whiskers dreams of you, it means something big is going to happen." She held out the *V.* "You can keep it."

RIIIINNNG. Saved by the bell, Victor thought.

Sidestepping around the girl, Victor headed into the school. Behind him, the girl watched him for a moment before opening up her backpack and slipping Mr. Whiskers inside. Victor might not believe her now, but he would. She was sure of it. Mr. Whiskers was never wrong. Something big was going to happen . . . soon.

Oblivious to the power of Mr. Whisker's "gifts," Victor headed to his favorite class—science. But when he got to the classroom, there was a new teacher standing at the front of the room. The man was tall, with a long face and deep-set eyes that peered out from behind glasses. His hair was slicked back and he had a thin mustache.

When everyone had taken their seats, he addressed the class. "I am Mr. Rzykruski," the man said in a thick, broken accent that sounded somewhere between a Russian spy and Dracula. "I will be your new science teacher. Apparently Mr. Holcum had an incident."

"He got hit by lightning," Elsa interrupted. The other kids in the classroom nodded. They had all heard the news but, based on the look on Mr. Rzykruski's face, he hadn't.

"Well. That is bad," he finally said. Seeing a chance to teach something, he went on. "But he did not get 'hit by' lightning. Lightning does not hit a person, the way one is hit by a baseball or a cabbage." In his seat, Nassor cringed, remembering just how it felt to be hit by a baseball.

Turning to the blackboard, Mr. Rzykruski began to illustrate his point. He drew a big cloud. "Lightning is simply electricity. The cloud is angry, yes, making a storm." He drew some more. "All the electrons are saying, 'I am leaving you. I am going to the land of opportunity.'"

As the kids watched, he drew land beneath the cloud. When he was done, Mr. Rzykruski went on. "The ground says, 'Yes, we need electrons trained in science just like you. Come! Come!' So both sides start to build a ladder." The teacher drew a stick figure. "This man, he comes to look at the storm. He does not see the invisible ladders. When the two ladders meet, BOOM! The circuit is complete and all of the electrons rush to the land of opportunity. This man is in the way. YIIIII!!!" Mr. Rzykruski let out a loud shriek, causing the students to jump in their seats. As the kids watched in wide-eyed wonder, he drew violent shock lines coming out of the stick figure. Turning back around, he saw the scared expressions on his students. Realizing he might have taken it too far, he cleared his throat. "But it is very rare to have such an incident," he finished.

For a moment, the room was silent. Then Victor slowly raised his hand. "But it's not rare. People get hit by . . ." He stopped and corrected himself. "Lightning happens to people all the time here."

The other students nodded. Victor was right. There was a thunderstorm almost every night in New Holland.

"My dad got hit twice," Bob said.

Toshiaki, Nassor, and Weird Girl added their two cents. "They built New Holland on an abandoned gold mine . . ." one of them said.

"I heard it was a cemetery," Toshiaki said, causing the classroom to fill with *oohs*.

"That's where they buried the miners," finished the other.

As everyone *oohed* and *ahhed*, Toshiaki shook

his head. "It's the windmill that does it," he said. Turning, he looked out the large window. In the distance, the windmill turned peacefully in the wind. It didn't *look* particularly menacing. But Toshiaki went on. "Turning, turning the air until the sky rages against the night."

The classroom filled with noise as everyone began to chatter excitedly. At the front of the room, Mr. Rzykruski tried to regain control. Clapping his hands together, he finally quieted the kids down. Perhaps he shouldn't have taught that particular lesson. "I want to announce the upcoming science fair," he said, changing the subject.

"Only seventh graders are allowed to enter the science fair," Nassor piped up. They were fourth graders.

Mr. Rzykruski shook his head angrily. "This is a ridiculous rule. There is no age limit on the making of a great scientist. Newton was five when he discovered, after eating a bad chicken dinner, that what goes down must come up."

As the other kids exchanged confused glances, Victor stared at his notebook. He had wanted to take part in the science fair, but he thought he would have to wait. Now he could participate! Maybe Mr. Whiskers's dream would come true. Maybe Victor would win and become a star scientist and no one would ever make fun of him again. Victor smiled at the thought.

As the bell rang, Victor jumped to his feet. Now he just needed to get home and invent something fantastic!

CHAPTER FOUR

While Victor had been busy learning about lightning, Sparky had been busy, too. He had found a tennis ball in the backyard and was chasing it back and forth. He would pick it up and toss it in the air, then chase after it barking wildly. He kept going until suddenly the ball rolled under a broken plank in the fence. Leaning down he pushed his nose through the hole. The ball was just out of reach. He wiggled and pushed himself but it was just too far. Then it disappeared!

Sparky let out a confused bark. Another dog barked in response. Jumping back. Sparky cocked his head. There wasn't usually a dog next door. He had barked at that fence plenty of times and never heard a bark back. Leaning down again, he began to sniff frantically. When he reached the broken plank, his nose sniffed faster—and then it touched another dog's nose!

What was happening?

Lying down so he could get a better view, Sparky looked through the hole. On the other side of the fence was a small, beautiful black poodle with a large poof of hair on her head. She was holding the tennis ball in her mouth. Seeing Sparky, the poodle dropped the ball. She wanted to play. But Sparky didn't understand. He rolled over onto his back and put his paws in the air submissively.

The poodle waited a moment to see if Sparky would get up. When he didn't, she grabbed the ball and trotted off. Popping up, Sparky watched her prance away. He had to find out more about this new neighbor of his. Maybe Victor would know when he got home.

Victor was making his way home as quickly as possible. But something—or rather, someone—was getting in his way. He had barely gotten through the school doors when Edgar Gore, "E" for short, had found him. The boy was short, with buckteeth and a small hunchback. He was a nice, but sometimes he tried a little too hard to make people like him.

"You'll be my partner for the science fair, right, Victor?" E begged, falling into step beside him. "Because you have to have a partner for the science fair and whoever's your partner is going to win. You know the most about science. So pick me as a partner. I have lots of ideas. We could make a death ray!"

Victor shook his head. "It says no death rays. See?" He held up the permission slip that Mr. Rzykruski had given them to get signed. On the paper was a long list of prohibited projects. It included everything from explosives to nuclear devices.

"Ah, man. I still want to do it," E said,

disappointed. But he wasn't about to give up. "C'mon. Who else would be your partner? You don't have friends and neither do I."

There was nothing Victor could say to that. E had a point. Victor Frankenstein had gained a reputation as being quite the loner, especially when it came to working in his lab. "I'm sorry Edgar," he said. "I just don't need a partner. I like to work alone." And with that, Victor headed home, leaving E behind.

Victor was thrilled to be taking part in the science fair. But there was one obstacle in his way—his father.

Mr. Frankenstein sat at the dining-room table staring at the permission slip Victor had given him a few moments earlier. In the kitchen, Victor's mother was putting the final touches on their dinner. Tonight was fondue night.

CHAPTER FOUR

As he read over the guidelines, Mr. Frankenstein's eyes narrowed. Nuclear devices? Explosives? What did the school administrators think their students were capable of creating? Slowly, he put the paper down and looked at his son. "Victor," he began, "have we talked about what I do for a living?"

Victor looked up from the plate of food his mother had put in front of him. "You're a travel agent," he replied.

"I sell dreams," his dad corrected. "I tell people, you can sail to Italy. You can do the hula in Hawaii."

This was nothing new to Victor. He had heard this speech before. "Will you sign my form?"

"I'm getting to that," his dad said. Picking up two fondue forks, he held them in front of his face. "In my job, sometimes you have people who don't want quite the same thing. Say the husband wants to play golf in Scotland, but the wife wants to pad-dle down the Amazon." He held the forks apart, as if they were the couple. "It's my job to help them meet halfway. Say, Scottsdale, Arizona."

That didn't make sense to Victor. "Nobody gets what they want," he pointed out.

His dad nodded. "Exactly! And wrong. They both get what they want because they *compromise*." He skewered a piece of beef with his fork. "You'd like to do this science fair. I'd like you to try a sport. Say, baseball. How do you choose?" Victor shrugged. "Guess what? You don't have to. No reason you can't do both. We meet in the middle. Everyone's happy." As he finished, he brought his two forks together and clinked them.

Victor stifled a groan. He had no choice. If he wanted to be in the science fair, it looked like he was playing baseball.

* * *

CHAPTER FOUR

The day after their conversation, Victor found himself in the outfield, nervously wiping sweat off his forehead. Baseball was bad enough, but when he had gotten to the field and seen his teammates, Victor knew it was only going to get worse. E, Nassor, Bob, and Toshiaki had been warming up. Toshiaki threw pitches to Nassor while E and Bob ran the bases. Watching over all of them was the coach—Mr. Frankenstein himself.

Victor had sighed and followed his dad's directions to take a spot out behind second base—well, he was pretty sure that was the base he was standing behind—and since then, he had just been waiting. And sweating.

Looking over, Mr. Frankenstein noticed the dazed look on his son's face. Jogging over, he put a hand on Victor's shoulder. "Look at what Toshiaki's doing. Keeping his eye on the target. Never losing his concentration."

Victor nodded absently, but he wasn't really listening. He was thinking about the science fair. "I want you to concentrate on your project for the science fair," Mr. Rzykruski had told them in class. That was no problem for Victor. He wanted to focus on the fair. If only baseball weren't in the way.

BOP!

Victor had been so lost in thought he didn't notice the fly ball coming right at him until it hit him on the head. He lifted his hand and felt the bump forming on his skull. Maybe he shouldn't be thinking about science on the baseball field. But Mr. Rzykruski's words kept running through his mind. "It's okay to fail as long as you keep trying," he had said. Maybe Victor could translate that to baseball.

The next day, when it was his turn at bat, Victor took a deep breath and waited for Toshiaki to pitch. As the ball came toward him, Victor brought his bat back and then SWING!! He let it fly. And missed. Three times in a row. Watching from the sidelines, Sparky let out a bark and went to get the pitcher's ball. At least the dog was having some fun.

Finally, it was time for an exhibition game. The science fair was scheduled for the following Friday. All Victor wanted to do was get through the game and then get home to work. His mom and Sparky had come out to cheer him on, along with Elsa and her dog, Persephone. Persephone was the dog Sparky had seen next door. He tried to wiggle closer to her as they watched the players take the field.

When it was his turn at bat, Victor nervously made his way to the plate. When he got there, he wiped his sweaty palms on his pants and tried to take a deep breath—but he almost choked. Looking up, he stared right into the eyes of Toshiaki.

The other boy raised the mitt to his chest as his left leg came up. He paused, staring down Victor. Then he pulled his arm back and threw—hard! The ball shot straight out of his hand, heading right toward Victor. Pulling his bat back, Victor closed his eyes and then swung through.

WHACK!

Victor had hit the ball! For a moment, he just stood there in shock. But then Sparky let out a bark and Victor began to run the bases. Meanwhile, Sparky had gotten so excited that he tore across the field, chasing the ball—which was now rolling through the outfield wildly. Bob tried to stop it, but he missed. The ball kept going, Sparky close behind. The ball rolled and rolled until finally it rolled right into the street. With a growl, Sparky pounced, catching the ball in his mouth. Turning, he looked back at Victor, wagging his little tail proudly.

Victor cheered and then started to call Sparky back. He shouldn't be on the road, Victor thought. A car could come by at any moment. Just then, to his horror, a car came careening around the corner. Victor shouted a warning to Sparky, but it was too late.

The car's brakes screeched. Someone let out a scream. Then there was a thump, and Sparky grew still. . . .

CHAPTER FIVE

The pet cemetery was quiet. Homemade and elaborate stone markers were spread throughout the large gated plot of land. Some had pictures of a beloved pet bird or dog, while others had names such as BUDDY and JACK etched on their surfaces.

As Victor and his mother watched, Mr. Frankenstein lowered a box into the ground under a new marker that simply read: SPARKY. Standing up, Mr. Frankenstein went to join his family. He put a hand gently on his son's shoulder. Victor didn't say anything. There was nothing to say. Sparky was gone.

Later that evening, Victor stood over his workbench, putting the finishing touches on his newly fixed projector. His eyes kept going to Sparky's treadmill, hoping he would see his best friend trotting along. But the treadmill was still. He felt his heart break even more.

With a sigh, he threaded the film through the reel and pressed PLAY. The screen lit up with an image of the Sparkysaurus attacking a Flying Turtle Monster. For a moment, Victor smiled. But just as quickly, the smile vanished and he once again felt only sadness. He lay his head on the workbench as a single tear slid down his cheek.

Later that night, Victor crawled into bed. Forgetting the day's events, he reached his hand down, waiting for Sparky to give him his good night lick. But there was no lick. Sparky wasn't there. Victor wondered, not for the first time, when it would ever feel normal again. Turning over, he stared up at the ceiling.

A few minutes later his parents came in, their faces creased with worry. Taking a seat on the edge of Victor's bed, Mrs. Frankenstein ran a gentle hand through her son's hair. Mr. Frankenstein sat down next to her.

"He was a great dog," Victor's mom said softly. "A great friend."

Mr. Frankenstein nodded. "The best dog a kid could have."

Victor didn't say anything. Exchanging a glance with her husband, Mrs. Frankenstein paused before saying, "When you lose someone you love, they never really leave you. They just move into a special place in your heart. He'll always be there, Victor."

Flipping on his side so that his back was to his parents, Victor let out a deep sigh. They didn't get it. "I don't want him in my heart," he said sadly. "I want him here, with me."

Leaning over, Mrs. Frankenstein gave her son a kiss on the cheek. Then she and her husband stood up to leave. At the door, she turned back. "If we could bring him back, we would," she said softly.

On his bed, Victor just stared at the wall.

There was nothing his parents could say to make it better. Sparky was gone. And he would never come back. He'd never play fetch with Victor or greet him at the door or get the morning paper. The stupid car had taken him away and now Victor was totally, and utterly, alone.

Even though he was sad and wanted to stay in bed forever, Victor's parents wouldn't let him. So the next day, he was back at school. He spent history writing Sparky's name over and over again in his notebook. During English, he wrote a story about Sparkysaurus. By the time he got to Science, he was despondent. As Mr. Rzykruski began his lecture on electricity, Victor opened up his notebook and began to doodle pictures of Sparky.

Looking over, Elsa noticed Victor's sad expression and his drawings. She wished there was something she could say to make him feel better. She would be the same way if something ever happened to Persephone. But Victor wouldn't look up. He wasn't even listening to Mr. Rzykruski. He was in serious mourning.

At the front of the room, the teacher continued to lecture, unaware of Victor's sadness. On his desk he had put a dead frog on display. He began to hook up an electrode to the frog's leg. "Just like lightning, the nervous system is electricity." He pointed to a small electric box next to the frog. The wire went from the frog's leg to the box. "Even after death, the wiring remains."

At the word death, Elsa looked over to see if Victor was okay. He hadn't even reacted.

Turning back to the front of the room, Elsa watched as Mr. Rzykruski flipped a switch on the electric box. There was a buzz and a spark and then . . . the frog's leg jumped, just as if it were alive!

Hearing the buzz, Victor looked up just in time to see the frog's newly animated leg. His heart began to beat faster. His eyes grew wider. He looked up at the frog and then down at his Sparky doodles and then back at the frog. Slowly, a smile spread across his face. He had an idea! A crazy, wild idea, but it might just work. Maybe Sparky wasn't gone forever after all!

As soon as school was over, Victor raced home. He had a lot to do. First, he grabbed various tools and equipment from the garage. Then he raided the kitchen, picking up a colander here, a pan there, an ironing board from the closet, and a few other household appliances. When he was satisfied he had everything he needed, he dropped it off upstairs. Next stop, the pet cemetery.

Victor waited until evening to sneak into the cemetery. A full moon shone down, making it

easy for Victor to find his way to Sparky's grave.
Making sure no one was looking, he began digging.
It was spooky, and several times Victor jumped at
an unexpected noise like an owl hooting or cat
screeching, but he kept digging. Finally, he was
done. Carefully, he opened the box they had put
Sparky in and picked up the wrapped bundle.
Placing Sparky in a wheelbarrow, Victor turned
and headed for home.

If getting Sparky had been scary, getting
past his parents was downright terrifying. Mr.
and Mrs. Frankenstein were having their weekly
movie night. They were cuddled up on the couch,
munching on popcorn. Crouching down, Victor
tiptoed behind the couch, heading toward the
stairs. Not watching where he was going, he
bumped into a lamp. He froze. The lamp teetered
and tottered, casting flickering light on the walls.
Victor waited, his heart pounding. If he got

caught . . . . Luckily, the lamp stopped rocking. Letting out a sigh of relief, Victor tiptoed quickly the rest of the way down the hall and up the stairs.

When he was safe in his attic laboratory, Victor got right to work. He placed his safety goggles over his eyes and shrugged on his lab coat. Then he looked down at his dog. Sparky had suffered some damage when the car hit him, but nothing Victor couldn't fix. As thunder began to boom outside, Victor started to stitch Sparky up. Then he grabbed some duct tape and made a few more adjustments. He was so close! Just a few more finishing touches and Sparky would be ready. Sifting through his toolbox, he tossed aside a slinky and then a hammer. He shook his head. Not what he was looking for. Finally he spotted his bucket of nuts and screws. Smiling, he grabbed two oversized bolts and attached them to Sparky's neck.

CHAPTER FIVE

BOOM! BOOM! BOOM! The thunder was growing louder as the storm got closer. Victor smiled. Everything was going according to plan!

Gently, Victor placed Sparky on his mother's ironing board and pushed it into the middle of the room. Knowing he would have to get Sparky outside somehow, Victor had built a retractable door into the roof that could be opened with a chain. A sudden flash of lightning illuminated Sparky. With a determined nod, Victor grabbed two balloons and an umbrella. Then he climbed up the ladder and out the door onto the roof. Another flash of lighting revealed a metal swing set. Victor took a moment to pat himself on the back. That had been the second hardest part of the plan after building the door—getting the swing up there and secured without his parent's noticing. Turning from the swing set, Victor raised a finger in the air to check the wind direction. North by Northwest.

Perfect. Taking the balloons, he attached them with a string to the umbrella. Then he attached the other end of the string to the metal swing set. It would be the perfect conductor.

Climbing back down the ladder, Victor double-checked his notes and equipment. The storm was almost directly on top of them. It was now or never. He had to get Sparky up onto the roof. He attached the ironing board to his homemade pulley system and then looked down at his dog one last time. "I love you, boy," he said softly and then gave him a gentle pat. If this didn't work . . .

Shaking off his doubts, Victor moved over to an old bike that he had mounted on a stand. Jumping on, he began pedaling furiously. Slowly, the ironing board lifted up toward the skylight. As the rain pounded down and lightning flashed, the board came to rest right under the metal swing set.

Now all Victor could do was wait.

Lifting his eyes, Victor silently urged on the lightning. C'mon, hit! Help me out! Please! he begged. He was so busy looking at the sky that he didn't even notice his hair beginning to stand on end. All the nuts and bolts he had dumped out were suddenly pulled upright. And then . . .

CRACK!

A jagged finger of lightning exploded out of the sky. It hit the top of the balloons, raced down the string, through the swing set, and finally slammed into the ironing board. There was a bright flash and a loud whine as the table was filled with a thousand volts of electricity. Then everything went silent.

Removing his goggles, Victor began cranking down the ironing board. When it was safely inside, he moved the board over to his workbench. Grabbing a stethoscope, he put the tips in his ears and the chest piece on Sparky. He listened. Nothing. He placed the scope on another part of Sparky and listened again. Still nothing. He did it one more time and still, nothing.

Laying his head down on the workbench, Victor absently rubbed Sparky's side as tears began to slide down his cheeks. "I'm sorry, boy," Victor sniffled. It hadn't worked. After all that, Victor still didn't have his dog back. His parents would probably be furious when they saw the swing set on the roof, and who knew if the neighbors had seen anything. If Mr. Burgemeister noticed, he was sure to tell Victor's parents. So he would be in trouble *and* never get another sloppy, scratchy lick from his best buddy. A lick that felt a lot like the one he was getting on his cheek right now . . .

What the heck!?

Victor sat up. There, still wrapped in blankets, but with his tail wagging happily, was Sparky! He looked a little worse for wear, but Victor didn't care. "You're alive!" he cried.

Sparky let out two loud barks and jumped into Victor's arms. His tail whipped back and forth as Sparky gave his boy wet, sloppy kisses. In fact, it was wagging so furiously that it came off and flew across the room. It landed with a little thud in the corner. Looking up, Victor saw the tail and then Sparky's bare backside. "I can fix that." Victor said. Then he went back to hugging his dog. Tail or no tail, it was great to have Sparky back.

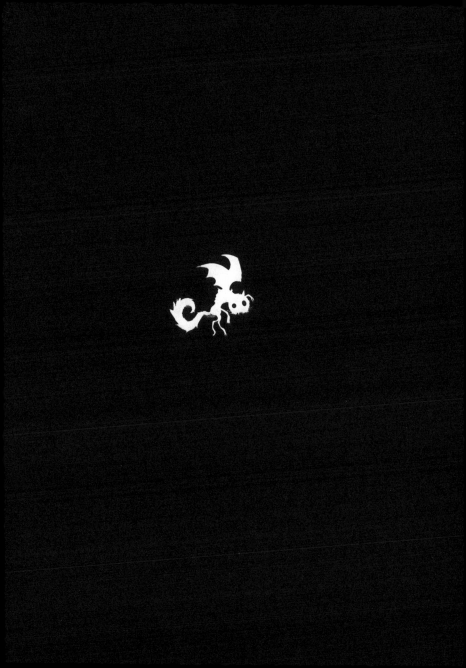

CHAPTER SIX

"**V**ictor! Breakfast!"

Up in the attic, Victor sat up and rubbed his eyes. He must have fallen asleep on the floor. Sparky was lying next to him.

"Victor?" his mother's voice shouted. "Are you up here?"

Hearing the sound of her footsteps on the attic stairs, Victor panicked. He couldn't let her see Sparky! Looking around he tried to find a place to hide his dog. For all his inventions and creations, he didn't have a lot of good covers. Finally his eyes settled on a big tin bucket that had been part of his monster-movie set. It would have to do. He grabbed the bucket and put it over Sparky just as the door opened and his mother peeked her head in.

"French toast or waffles?" she asked.

"Waffles," Victor answered. The sooner he could get her out of there the better. But it had been the wrong answer.

"Then I'll need my waffle iron back, Mr. Director." She scanned the room, looking for the iron. Noticing it right by the tin bucket that was currently hiding Sparky, she walked over to pick it up. The bucket moved. Turning, Mrs. Frankenstein gave her son a confused look.

"Uh, it's my science project," Victor said, thinking quickly. "It's a robot."

"A robotic bucket?" his mother asked, confused. Victor nodded. "For mopping, I suppose?" He nodded again.

Picking up the waffle iron, Victor's mom gave the bucket one last look. "Maybe when you're finished, you'll let me use it." Then, with a smile, she headed back downstairs.

Victor raced over and shut the door behind her. Then he turned around and leaned against it, letting out a deep breath. That had been too close for comfort. He took the bucket off Sparky and scratched the dog behind his ears. "Sorry, boy," he said. "But I can't let anyone know about you. They might not understand. You need to stay here today."

Giving his dog one last pat, Victor turned and left the room, shutting the door behind him. Sparky heard the lock click and the sound of Victor's footsteps. Then it was silent in the attic. Lying down, Sparky put his head on his paws and waited.

Sparky had every intention of being a good dog while Victor was at school. He jumped on his treadmill for a quick run. When he got thirsty he had a drink. It bothered him a little when the water leaked out his stitches, but he got used to it pretty quickly. Everything was going fine. And then the cat showed up.

MEOW!

Mr. Whiskers was perched in the open attic window. Seeing Sparky, the cat hissed.

Letting out a bark, Sparky jumped on a chair, then up onto the workbench. Rocking back on his hind legs, Sparky lunged up, up, up, right at the cat! Hissing, the cat slipped out of his reach—but not before Sparky had landed on the roof outside. Digging his claws into the shingles, he tried to stabilize himself. But the roof was just too steep. With a yelp, he slid down, down, down, landing with a *thump* in the bushes right below the Frankensteins' picture window.

In the living room, Mrs. Frankenstein was vacuuming while reading a romance novel. Out of the corner of her eye she thought she saw something. But when she looked over, there was nothing there. Shrugging, she went back to her reading.

Meanwhile, Sparky emerged from the bushes

and shook himself off. When he went to walk,
though, he noticed that his back leg was dislo-
cated. He shook it a few times but that didn't work.
Finally, he rolled over on the grass and the leg
popped back into place. Much better.

But Sparky now had a bigger problem. How was
he going to get back into the house? He looked up
at the attic window. There was no way he could go
back in the way he came out. Sparky was just about
to try the front door when Mr. Frankenstein's car
pulled into the driveway. So the front door was out
of the question.

HISS!

Turning around, Sparky found himself face-
to-face with Mr. Whiskers. It let out another hiss
and then raced into Mr. Burgemeister's yard.
Forgetting all about getting inside, Sparky let out
a bark and began chasing the cat.

Sparky chased Mr. Whiskers through Mr.

Burgemeister's prized tulips, crushing all of them.
Mr. Whiskers jumped on a pink flamingo and
paused there until the one-legged bird toppled
over. When the cat leaped into the bushes, Sparky
followed. Everywhere the cat went, Sparky went,
too. Even when the cat vanished, Sparky kept
going. He ran down the street past two mothers
walking. One of them was pushing a stroller with
a baby inside. Seeing the dog, the baby began
to clap. But when Sparky got closer, the baby
screamed. Sparky quickly ran away, leaving the
mother to wonder what was wrong with her child.

Soon, Sparky found himself racing past
Victor's school. He was tempted to try and find his
boy, but he knew Victor wanted him to stay home.
Then he saw one of the kid's from Victor's class.
He was pretty sure his name was E. Or Edgar. Or
something. Stopping, Sparky wagged his tail.

E had been on his way to the nurse's office

after a small run-in with a maypole in gym class. He was shuffling along, mumbling about dances and maypoles when he heard the sound of paws on pavement. Looking up, he saw . . . Sparky? E did a double take. Sparky was supposed to be dead! As Sparky raced off, E's eyes narrowed. Something was going on. And E was going to find out just what it was.

Sparky was exhausted. He had finally made it home, but now he had to wait until Victor got back before he could go inside. He flopped down in the shade of a big tree to rest. As he lay there, a fly buzzed by, trying to land on him. With a flick of his tongue, Sparky ate it.

He had just closed his eyes when his nostrils began to twitch. He smelled something good. Looking over he saw Persephone. She was looking at him oddly, as though she knew something wasn't quite right. Rolling over on his belly, he waited for her to come closer. Persephone inched closer. Then she leaned down and sniffed. Her nose touched one of the bolts on Sparky's neck.

ZAAPPP!

A shock of electricity knocked her down. She quickly popped back up, no worse for wear, and now sporting a white streak through her trademark black head poof à la the Bride of Frankenstein. Sparky let out a sigh.

Finally, Victor came home. Following him up the stairs as quietly as possible, Sparky snuck into the attic and ran into a corner. Victor began calling his name. Sparky waited until Victor's back was turned and then he ran over and nudged his leg, as though he had been inside all day.

"There you are! Good boy!" Victor said happily. He leaned down and gave Sparky a hug. "Sorry you had to stay here alone all day."

CHAPTER SIX

Sparky just wagged his tail.

"You're a little low," Victor said, noticing that Sparky seemed tired. "Are you hungry, boy?"

Sparky barked.

Quickly, Victor ran an extension cord from the wall to a socket on Sparky's thigh. Plugging it in, Sparky's eyes began to glow. Leaving his dog to recharge, Victor began to fiddle with his equipment. He heard the doorbell ring downstairs but ignored it until his mother called out, "Victor, your friend is here."

Running downstairs to the kitchen, Victor found his mother baking and E waiting for him at the kitchen bar.

As his mother stayed close by, Victor asked quietly, "Edgar, what are you doing here?"

"I know," E replied.

"Oh," Victor said.

"I know," E repeated.

This was getting weird. If E knew that Victor couldn't work on their project, what was he doing at his house? "Know what?" he asked finally.

"You know," E answered.

"No." This was getting downright annoying.

E narrowed his eyes. "I think I know what you know I know."

"I don't know what you think I know," Victor said, shaking his head, "but I don't know it."

"Your dog is alive," E said, ending the confusion.

Victor gulped and pulled the door shut so his mom wouldn't hear. "That's impossible!"

E nodded his head. "I know, but you did it." When Victor didn't say anything, E went on, "So show me how, or I'll tell everyone."

It looked like Victor didn't have a choice. He was going to have to show E how to bring an animal back to life. He just hoped it worked again . . . or else he was going to be in a lot of trouble.

CHAPTER SEVEN

The first thing he had to do, Victor told E, was get an animal. Since E didn't have a pet, he headed to the nearest pet store. Looking around he saw some hamsters, a guinea pig or two, and a snake. They could all work, but E was looking for something in particular. Then he saw the fish tanks.

"Can I help you young man?" the pet store owner asked, noticing E standing in front of the goldfish.

"I'd like to buy a fish." Then he pointed to the one he wanted. It was floating belly-up at the top of the tank.

The pet store owner gave E an odd look. Then he shrugged. A sale was a sale.

Smiling, E took the plastic bag with his fish. Next step, bringing it back to life.

Back at Victor's house, E plopped the dead fish into a small jar of water. While the other boy was at the store, Victor attached electrodes from the jar to the metal table. Curious, Sparky jumped onto the table and pushed at the jar with his nose.

"Down, boy," Victor commanded. He didn't know what would happen if Sparky got zapped with another bolt of electricity.

Outside, night had fallen. Storm clouds had been amassing all day, and now a big storm was raging. Once again, Victor opened the attic roof. Then he hopped on his bike and began pedaling as fast as he could to rise the metal table into the sky. When it was secure, Victor got off his bike and waited.

"What do we do now?" E asked, just as his hair stood on end.

Victor knew what that meant. Grabbing E, he threw him to floor just as there was a loud CRACK!

Lightning surged down the lightning rod Victor had hooked up to the metal table. With a spark, the water inside the jar began to bubble. It lasted a few seconds and then, just as quickly as it had started, the bubbling stopped.

When he was sure it was safe, Victor brought the metal table back down into the room. Together, he and E peered into the metal jar. The fish was gone.

"What happened to it?" E asked, confused. "What did you do?"

"I don't know," Victor replied. "It *should* have worked." Leaning in, Victor tried to take a closer look. The water rippled. That was interesting. . . .

Victor had a hunch. Grabbing a flashlight he had rigged with various lenses that could spin in front of the bulb, Victor dimmed the overhead lights. He looked through all the colored lenses, settling on one that was slightly purple. Flipping on the flashlight, he aimed it at the jar of water. For a moment, it just looked like water.

And then, a fish skeleton swam past. When it

moved out of the ray of light, it disappeared.

"It's invisible!" Victor said in wonder. "An invisible goldfish!"

But *why* had the fish turned invisible when it came back to life when Sparky was visible as he was always had been? Victor would have to look into it.

A little later, after the storm had passed, Victor walked E to the front door. "You can't tell anyone. You understand that, right? Not until we figure out how it works."

E looked down at the apparently empty jar in his hand and nodded. "Okay, okay!"

"Promise!" Victor demanded.

"Promise," E repeated.

Unfortunately, E was a horrible secret-keeper. No sooner had he left Victor's house than he made his way to Toshiaki's. He couldn't wait to show the cool boys his invisible fish. Toshiaki, Bob and Nassor would beg him to be their friend. They'd save him a seat in the cafeteria and pick him first for their teams. He would have not just one friend, but four. It would be perfect.

But there was a small problem. Victor had kept the special flashlight.

"How are we supposed to see an invisible goldfish?" Toshiaki asked, waving his own regular flashlight back and forth in front of the jar. The water looked empty.

E racked his brain. "Put your finger in?" He suggested. "Maybe you can feel it."

Toshiaki and Bob traded looks. Was E trying to prank them? With a shrug, Bob put his finger in. It wasn't like an empty jar of water could hurt them, right?

Nothing happened.

He swirled his finger around the whole jar.

Still nothing.

And then . . .

"Aaah!" Bob cried, yanking his finger out of the water. "It bit me!"

"Let me see it!" Toshiaki said, grabbing the jar from E and pressing the flashlight up against the glass. On the wall behind the jar a giant goldfish shadow appeared. It had the shape of a regular goldfish but its teeth were giant, like something a dinosaur would have in its mouth.

Taking the jar back, E screwed the lid on tight. "You can't tell anybody," he said, echoing Victor's earlier words. "It's our science-fair project."

"Yeah, well our science-fair project is even cooler," Bob said, nursing his finger.

"What is it?" E asked, curious.

Bob and Toshiaki exchanged a look. That was an excellent question. Technically, they didn't have a very cool project, but E didn't need to know that.

"It's double top secret," Toshiaki said, ending the conversation.

After E left, Bob and Toshiaki went out to the garage. Their "project" was set up on a workbench. In a big aquarium were a bunch of popsicle sticks. They were supposed to be islands—for sea creatures. That was their big, double top secret project.

"We gotta come up with something better," Bob said.

"I know," Toshiaki said.

Bob began to look panicked. *The science fair is in two days!!"* he shouted.

"I know," Toshiaki repeated.

"You're the smart one," Bob pointed out.

"Lemme think," Toshiaki snapped. He knew he was the smartest one in the group. But what could he possibly create in two days that could beat an invisible, giant-toothed goldfish?

* * *

The next afternoon, E was unlocking his bike to go home when a shadow fell across him. Looking up, he saw Nassor. The other boy was staring at him with his sinister eyes.

"Toshiaki says you have an invisible fish," Nassor said.

E gulped. "No, he doesn't," he said nervously.

"So you don't?" Nassor hedged.

"I didn't say that."

Nassor shook his head. He knew E was lying. "Toshiaki says it's your science-fair project."

"If it was, I couldn't tell you," E said, trying to back away from the other boy.

"So it isn't? Or it is?"

E was getting more and more nervous. Nassor scared him. "No. Yes." He shook his head. "I'm confused."

Nassor grinned evilly. He had E just where he wanted him. "Do you have an invisible fish?" he asked.

Finally, E gave in. He couldn't take any more torture. Reaching into his backpack he pulled out the jar of water and unscrewed the lid. He told Nassor to dip his finger in and swish it around. But when Nassor did it, nothing happened.

"It's just water," Nassor said. "There's nothing there."

E dipped his own finger in, feeling around for the toothy goldfish. He swished and he swished but there was nothing there. That was weird. It couldn't have escaped. So where did it go?

Nassor had had enough. "I don't know what kind of game you and Victor are playing, but that trophy will be mine."

"What trophy?" E asked.

"The science fair," Nassor answered. "There's a trophy." He leaned in close, pushing his buck-teeth into E's face. "And I intend to win it."

E gulped. This wasn't good.

CHAPTER EIGHT

E had to find Victor—he would know what to do. Hopping on his bike E raced away from school. By the time he caught up with Victor, he was out of breath.

"Something's wrong with my fish," he gasped.

Victor stopped his bike. "What is it?" he asked.

E held a hand to his chest, trying to catch his breath before he went on. Finally he said, "It's not there anymore."

"Maybe it hopped out," Victor suggested, not really worried. "Did you have the lid on?"

"Yes!" E exclaimed. There was no way E was going to tell Victor that he had shown the fish to Toshiaki, Bob, *and* Nassor. He had promised he wouldn't tell anyone. "Ever since . . . since I left your house. I mean, it was there when I went to bed."

Victor was silent as he pondered the

possibilities. He had done all the calculations correctly. And Sparky was still fine. So what could have gone wrong? Was the lightning a different voltage? Did fish react differently to the experiment?

Nervously, E waited for Victor to say something. When he didn't, E gulped. He had an idea of what could have happened. But he was scared to say it out loud. But when Victor still hadn't said anything, E took a chance. "I'm thinking," he began, "maybe they don't last. Maybe they're like fireworks. They're only there for a little bit and then they're gone."

Victor's eyes grew wide. Sparky! He had to get home!

Without even a good-bye to E, Victor raced away. When he arrived at his house, Victor ran upstairs to the attic. Opening the door, his eyes went right to where he had left Sparky tied up. The rope was still there, attached to his dog's collar. But Sparky was gone!

"No!" Victor cried out. How could this have happened? Why hadn't he made sure to check his calculations?

WOOF!

At the sound of the bark, Victor whipped his head around. Then he let out a huge sigh of relief. There, happily—and visibly—drinking out of his water bowl, was Sparky. Water trickled out of his stitches, but he didn't notice. Pausing to scratch his ear, however, Sparky was surprised when it came right off.

Rushing over to him, Victor picked Sparky up and hugged him close. Sparky wasn't quite sure what all the fuss was about, but he happily licked Victor's face and wagged his tail.

Noticing his ear, Victor hugged his best friend closer. "Don't worry," he said. "I can fix that, too." One ear or two, Victor was just happy Sparky was still there.

Ever since E had shown them his invisible fish, Toshiaki and Bob had been trying to come up with a project that was better. It was not easy. They had tried making a volcano that erupted. But they had used ketchup as the lava—and when it exploded all over Bob's kitchen, his mother had not been happy. Toshiaki's parents weren't thrilled when they brought home a dozen rats. The rodents had escaped when Toshiaki tried to teach them to go through a maze. They had only been able to find eleven.

But finally, Toshiaki had come up with an idea. Now they just needed to test it.

"Are you sure this is going to work?" Bob asked nervously. He and Toshiaki were on the roof of Toshiaki's house. Bob was wearing a modified backpack. Nine big soda bottles were lashed to it, their caps pointing down. A pull-string was attached to each of the caps. Behind him, Toshiaki was shaking a tenth soda bottle.

"No," Toshiaki replied, making Bob even more nervous. "That's why it's called an experiment. We have to collect data."

"But do we have to collect it on *me*?" Bob whined.

Placing the last bottle on the backpack, Toshiaki ignored his friend's complaining. "Ready?" he asked.

"No," Bob said.

Toshiaki began the countdown anyway. "Ten. Nine. Eight."

"We could use a test dummy or something," Bob suggested.

"Seven. Six. Five." Toshiaki counted.

"Computer simulation?"

Toshiaki shook his head. "Four. Three. Two . . . One!" He pulled the strings attached to the soda caps. Foamy liquid blasted out of the bottles, spraying the ground. Bob suddenly found himself hovering—albeit in fits and starts—in the air.

"It's working!" he screamed. "It's working!"

Grabbing his video camera to document their success, Toshiaki began recording. Looking through the lens, he noticed that the soda bottles were growing empty. The last little bit dropped out of the bottles and then . . . Bob dropped out of the sky. He thumped down onto the roof. Once, twice. Then, as Toshiaki watched, Bob thumbed right over the edge of the roof. He landed on the ground with a thud, his arm bent.

Toshiaki gulped. This was going to be hard to explain.

As soon as Bob's mother saw her son lying on the ground, she called an ambulance. When she found out *how* he had broken his arm, she called the school. And when the principal found out a student had hurt himself working on a science project, he called the mayor. Something had to be done.

Mayor Burgemeister called a town meeting. When everyone was gathered in the school assembly room, he walked up to the podium that had been set up on the stage. He spied the microphone and narrowed his eyes. It was far too low. As he attempted to adjust it, a loud squeal of feedback echoed through the room. The audience clasped their hands to their ears. When the noise faded away, Mr. Burgemeister cleared his throat and began. "As mayor of New Holland, you have entrusted me with your safety. So I can't sit idly by while a teacher endangers our children." He paused to look at his notes and then went on. "Mr. Ryzk . . . krusekishi . . . krysk . . ." The mayor stumbled over the teacher's name, struggling with the unusual spelling.

Standing up in the crowd, Bob's mother interrupted the mayor, shouting, "He's a menace!" There were nods and murmurs of agreement from the other parents attending the assembly. Sitting next to her, his arm in a sling, Bob looked sheepish.

But not everyone agreed. "Mayor," Mr. Frankenstein said, standing up as well, "I can tell you that our son, Victor, is just crazy about the new teacher. Thinks he's great."

"Have you looked through this 'science' book they're using?" another father asked, ignoring the positive feedback. "Apparently, Pluto isn't good enough to be a planet anymore. This guy comes along and rewrites the rules."

Another mother stood up. "My Cynthia has been asking all sorts of strange questions. About things I've never even heard of!"

Mr. Frankenstein tried to reason with the

parents again. "We should at least give the man the chance to explain himself."

The science teacher had been lingering in the back of the room, listening to the accusations. Finally, he walked up to the podium. Looking around the room, he smiled. Unfortunately, his smile was a bit, well, creepy, and he was met with a sea of stony faces. "I think the confusion here is that you are all very ignorant," he began. The faces grew stonier and Mr. Rzykruski tried again. "Is this the right word, 'ignorant'? I mean simple. Unenlightened."

The audience was beginning to squirm in their seats. They had come here to do the picking, not get picked on.

Mr. Rzykruski forged ahead, each word getting him into deeper and deeper trouble. "You do not understand science, so you are afraid of it. Like a dog is afraid of thunder or balloons." As he spoke, his accent got a little clearer and his voice grew stronger. He was on a roll. "To you, science is magic and witchcraft, because you have such small minds. I cannot make your heads bigger, but your children's heads—" He paused, looking for the right words. "I can take them and crack them open. This is what I try to do. To get at their brains."

When he finished the room was silent. Mr. Rzykruski looked pleased, unaware that he had only added fuel to the parents' fire. Saying thank you, he left the stage.

If the parents had anything to do with it, he would be leaving the school as well.

CHAPTER NINE

The next day Mr. Rzykruski's students filed into class and took their seats. Just before the bell rang, the school's gym teacher walked in. Boys and girls began to murmur in confusion. Taking a place in front of the desk, she waited for the class to quiet down.

Victor raised his hand. "Where's Mr. Rzykruski?" he asked.

"He's not here today," the gym teacher answered.

"Is he coming back?" Toshiaki asked.

The gym teacher shrugged. "All I know is, I'll be teaching the class for the rest of the semester." She turned and began to erase the messy blackboard. Behind her the kids exchanged confused glances and began to whisper to one another. What was going on? What had happened last night at the assembly?

"Do you know anything about science?" Elsa finally questioned.

"I know more than you do," the teacher replied, giving her a look that said "stop bugging me."

"Mr. Rzykruski knew a lot," Bob said. He felt partly responsible for the gym teacher's presence. But he wasn't about to admit that he had gotten Mr. Rzykruski in trouble.

The gym teacher was getting annoyed with all the questions. She was here to do her job. She would much rather be preparing a game of kick ball or practicing drills on the soccer field. "Well, sometimes knowing too much is the problem," she finally responded, her voice chilly.

For a moment, no one said anything. But everyone was thinking about the same thing—the science fair. Was it still going to happen?

"Oh, it's still on," the gym teacher said when Victor asked. "So get cracking and may the best person win. Also class, besides death rays, explosives, and nuclear devices, I'm adding rodents and reptiles to the no-go list."

With her new rules issued, she began to write the day's lesson on the blackboard. Behind her, the students were silent. They were beginning to really miss Mr. Rzykruski.

"I can't believe I broke my arm for nothing," Bob said later that day. He, Nassor, and Toshiaki were hanging out behind the school. They weren't happy that the science fair was still going to happen. Without Mr. Rzykruski around, they figured the fair would be cancelled and they wouldn't have to come up with a project. But now the fair was two days away and they still had nothing.

"None of us are going to win," Bob went on. "E has an invisible fish!"

Nassor shook his head. "No he doesn't. You fell for a parlor trick."

"You're saying he faked it?" Toshiaki asked. He had been there. He had seen the goldfish shadow on the wall. Could he really have been fooled by E.?

Just then, E came around the corner. Spotting him, the boys walked over and formed a circle around the lone boy. He panicked and tried to get away but there was nowhere to go. He was trapped.

"That fish you showed us, was it real?" Toshiaki asked.

E gulped. "It was!" he cried. "And it was dead, too." He brought a hand to his mouth. Oops! He wasn't supposed to have said that. But he was nervous and when he got nervous he spoke without thinking.

Nassor narrowed his eyes. "You brought an animal back from the dead?"

"No, Victor did. With lightning and BOOM!

And SSS!!" E replied, pulling his hair up as though lightning had made it stand on end.

"Impossible," Nassor and Toshiaki said at the same time.

E shook his head. "I swear! I mean he already brought back his dog." Oops! He had done it again! He had promised Victor he wouldn't say anything. If Victor found out that E had cracked under the pressure he was going to be so mad!

"He brought back Sparky?" the boys asked. E had no choice but to nod. The other boys exchanged a look. If E was telling the truth, it meant that Victor was going to win the science fair, hands down. Unless . . . they could think of something that was bigger and better than bringing a dog back to life.

Victor was worried. Not only was his favorite teacher leaving, he still didn't understand what had gone wrong with the fish experiment. If the fish could disappear that easily, did that mean Sparky would disappear eventually?

He knew the only person who could help him was his science teacher. So as soon as school was over, he began to search for Mr. Rzykruski. He had to be around somewhere.

Finally, Victor found the teacher packing up his car in the school parking lot. He was stuffing the car full of odds and ends from his classroom. The car was as strange as Mr. Rzykruski himself and already looked to be full.

"I can't believe the gym teacher is in charge of the science fair," Victor said, walking up behind Mr. Rzykruski. "She's not even interested in science."

Turning around, Mr. Rzykruski smiled at his favorite student. He would miss Victor. "Back home, everyone is scientist," he said. He held up his hand and began counting on his fingers. "Physicist, chemist, biologist. My plumber, he wins the Nobel Prize. Your country does not make enough scientists. *You* should be a scientist."

"Nobody likes scientists," Victor said sadly.

Mr. Rzykruski nodded. The boy had a point. "They like what science gives them, but not the questions—no, not the questions that science asks."

Victor's heart began to beat faster. It was now or never. "*I* have a question," he said.

"That is why you are scientist," Mr. Rzykruski replied.

Smiling a little, Victor gathered his courage. He trusted Mr. Rzykruski. And he was the smartest man he knew. If he couldn't help Victor, no one could. He had to ask, for Sparky's sake. "I was doing my experiment, my project, and the first time it worked great," Victor began. "But the next time it didn't. I mean it sort of worked, but then it didn't. And I don't know why."

Mr. Rzykruski was silent for a moment, taking in his student's words. Then he spoke. "Then maybe you never really understood it the first time. People think science is here . . ." He tapped Victor's head. Then he tapped his heart. "But it is also here. The first time, did you love your experiment?"

Victor thought back to that terrible day when he lost Sparky. And then the hope he had felt when he found a way to bring him back. He remembered the lightning and the flash and then the waiting and the wishing. And then he remembered hugging Sparky, so scared it hadn't worked. And finally, he remembered the joy when Sparky licked his face. Of course he had loved his experiment. Sparky was his best friend.

"Yes," he answered simply.

"And the second time?" Mr. Rzykruski asked.

This time when Victor thought about the fish and E and the lightning crackling, he didn't feel worry or hope or joy. He remembered just wishing that E had never seen Sparky. And he remembered thinking that if he helped E, maybe the boy would leave him alone. "No," he said. "I just wanted it to be over."

Mr. Rzykruski nodded. Just as he suspected. "You changed the variables," he explained.

"I was doing it for the wrong reason," Victor said, understanding washing over him.

"Science is not good or bad, Victor," Mr. Rzykruski said, shutting the trunk of his car. "But it can be used both ways. That is why you must always be careful." Holding out his hand, he and Victor shook. Then the teacher got in his car and drove off.

Watching him leave, Victor felt a huge weight

come off his shoulders. He knew what had gone wrong with the fish now. But he had loved Sparky when he brought him back. And he would love him forever. So Sparky would be safe, just as long as nobody found out about him . . .

CHAPTER TEN

I t was Dutch Day in New Holland. The event that Mayor Burgemeister had been preparing for all year and the event that gave the town citizens an excuse to break out their lederhosen and wooden shoes. Downtown, the main square had been completely transformed. Storefronts were decorated with pictures of canals and tulips. The street was lined with more tulips and booths set up to sell Van Gogh replicas and mini windmills. A few carnival rides had been set up on the outskirts of the square and several oompah bands meandered about, oomping as loudly as they could. Everyone was in a festive mood as the final touches were put up for the big party later that night.

In her kitchen, Mrs. Frankenstein was busy looking through her recipe book. She needed to find something perfect to make for the bake sale. Carrot cake? No, not Dutch enough. Stroopwafel?

No, too Dutch. Chocolate cherry cheese cupcakes? Perfect! She even had everything she needed in the house.

Turning on the oven, she began to mix the ingredients. She beat the eggs and stirred in the oil and sugar. Then she added some flour and cocoa and finished with cream cheese and a few spoonfuls of jam. But when she went to put the mix into the muffin tin, she couldn't find it. She searched through her cabinets, pulling out pan after pan, but none of them were the right one.

Frustrated, she sat back on her heels. Where could her muffin tin have gone?

And then she knew—Victor.

Up in the attic, Sparky was taking a nap when he heard the doorknob begin to rattle. Jumping to his feet, he began to look for a place to hide.

On the other side of the attic door, Mrs.

Frankenstein turned the knob a few more times. It was locked. Pulling a pin out of her hair, she fiddled with it, bending and twisting until it was an eerily accurate-looking key. Apparently, Victor wasn't the only creative member of the family. Placing it into the lock, she wiggled a few times and then the door unlocked with a POP and swung open.

Walking inside, she began to search for her muffin tin. She looked through the various piles of odds and ends. She sidestepped the movie projector and Sparky's treadmill. Finally, she spotted the tin. It was part of an elaborate set Victor had created for one of his movies. The tin was standing on its end, acting as a wall. Bending down, Mrs. Frankenstein grabbed the tin.

Sparky was right behind it! He stood, frozen, trying not to get noticed.

Mrs. Frankenstein had been distracted by

Victor's chalkboard. Turning her back to Sparky she walked over for a closer look. Her eyes narrowed as she made out their house. And then her head cocked when she saw the roof wide open. Their roof didn't open, did it?

Taking a closer look she saw that there seemed to be something attached to the ceiling—a single chain hanging down. Curious, Mrs. Frankenstein gave the chain a tug. Instantly, the attic filled with the sound of whizzing and clicking. As she watched in awe, the roof spread open and a long lightning rod stretched up into the sky. Mrs. Frankenstein had never seen anything like this. Had Victor done all this himself? As she continued to watch, a fan switched on and fabric began to swirl, creating static. The static created an arc of lightning which began to climb up the rod and outside. With a gasp, Mrs. Frankenstein dropped the muffin tin, sending it clattering to the floor.

CHAPTER TEN

Woof!

Behind her, Sparky had jumped at the sound of the tin hitting the floor. Out of pure gut instinct he had barked—and given himself away.

Hearing the bark, Mrs. Frankenstein turned. Spotting Sparky, her eyes grew wide.

"AHHHHHHHHHHHHHHHHHHHH!"

She let out a scream. Petrified, Sparky turned and began to race out the door when he crashed into a nearby mirror, the impact causing it to splinter.

When he looked up, Sparky saw his reflection—and understood why Mrs. Frankenstein was screaming. Huge bolts protruded from his neck. Scars covered his body and face. He was grotesque, broken. Sparky was . . . a monster. Horrified at what he saw, Sparky jumped out the window and ran off into the night.

* * *

Victor knew he was in trouble. But he didn't care. "We have to find Sparky before someone else does!" he cried.

His father was pacing back and forth across the living room while Victor sat on the couch with his mother. Mrs. Frankenstein had a cold compress pressed to her forehead. She was still recovering from her earlier run-in with Sparky.

"Now, let's not get ahead of ourselves," Mr. Frankenstein said. "What you did is a very serious thing, young man."

"You said yourself: if you could bring back Sparky, you would."

Victor's dad threw his hands up in the air. "That was different," he said, "because we couldn't!" On the couch, Victor looked down at his hands and didn't say anything. His father went on. "Crossing the boundary between life and death—it's very . . . unsettling."

As his father droned on, tears welled up in Victor's eyes. "I just wanted my dog back," he said, sniffling.

His mom reached out and rubbed his back. "I know," she said gently.

"You *can't* get rid of Sparky!" Victor cried, shrugging off his mother's touch.

Mr. and Mrs. Frankenstein exchanged looks. They had discussed this before Victor got home. It would be cruel to hurt Sparky now when he seemed, well, alive. So they had come up with a compromise.

"Whenever Sparky . . . um . . . passes on," Victor's mom said, "you're going to need to let him go. No more bringing him back from the dead. Understood?"

Victor let out a sigh. It wasn't exactly what he wanted to hear. But he would take it for now. He would just figure out a way to prevent Sparky from ever passing on. He nodded yes.

His father smiled and clapped his hands. Good! "Now let's go find your dog!" They couldn't let Sparky run around free. Who knew how people would react if they saw him—bolts, stitches, and all.

CHAPTER ELEVEN

naware of the happenings going on next door, Mayor Burgemeister put the finishing touches on his Dutch Day dance outfit. When he was sure he looked perfect, he stepped out the front door, making one last adjustment to his sash. It read MAYOR across the front. He wanted to make sure that it was centered perfectly.

"Elsa!" he called over his shoulder. "We'll be late!"

A moment later, Elsa emerged. She was dressed head to toe in traditional Dutch attire, including lederhosen and a blond wig pulled into pigtails. Even Persephone had been dragged into the costume and was covered in garlands. Both girl and dog looked miserable.

"You know, a lot of girls would kill to be in your place," the mayor said when he saw her frown.

"I'd welcome death," Elsa replied in a monotone.

Just as Burgemeister was about to launch into a lecture on gratefulness and respect, he and Elsa spotted the Frankensteins. They were wandering around their house waving flashlights.

"Spar-ky!" Mrs. Frankenstein called. "Spar-ky!" The beam of her flashlight swept right past Elsa and Mr. Burgemeister, stopped, and then slowly swept back as Mrs. Frankenstein realized she had an audience.

"Wasn't that the boy's dog?" the mayor asked suspiciously.

"Yes," Mrs. Frankenstein said, trying to sound nonchalant.

"The one who died?" Burgemeister needled.

"Yes," she answered again.

Burgemeister's beady eyes narrowed. "So . . . what are you doing?" he asked.

Seeing that his wife was in trouble, Mr. Frankenstein came over. He smiled at his neighbor as though this was something that happened every night. "It's a game we play," he explained. From behind the house, they all heard Victor call out Sparky's name.

"You play a game in which you look for a boy's dead dog?" Mr. Burgemeister asked, trying to make sure he understood correctly.

The Frankensteins nodded.

"Explains a lot," Burgemeister said, shrugging. He had always known they were a weird family. This odd "game" just proved it.

Mr. Burgemeister turned to lock the front door. After all, he couldn't be late to his own town celebration. Just then, Victor ran past. "I'm going to check out the school and the park," he told his parents, not even bothering to slow down. "You guys do the town square, okay?"

"Got it!" his dad called back.

Elsa's eyes followed Victor as he ran away.

He was acting really strange. Even stranger than usual. And all this talk of Sparky? And the weird game? She thought she had heard E say something to the boys in class about Sparky coming back to life. Could that be true? Could Sparky really be alive? And if he was, where had he gone?

With questions racing through her mind, Elsa followed her uncle down the walkway. It looked like she would have to wait and find out just what was going on. . . .

Downtown, the Dutch Day celebration was in full swing. Almost the entire town had gathered beneath the large tent set up in the main square. On an elevated stage the oompah band was playing classic Dutch songs while women in wooden shoes performed a festive dance. People clapped and moved with the music, caught up in the festive mood.

Not everyone was enjoying the celebration. Poor Sparky was trying to make his way unseen through the town. But everywhere he turned, there was something to scare him. A marching band paraded past. Sparky leaped out of the way. The oompah band made a loud oompah. Sparky jumped. Finally seeing a way out through the crowd, he ran as fast as he could, his tail tucked between his legs. For a moment, he thought he heard someone calling his name, but he kept running. He had to get away from all those people.

Sparky didn't stop running until he found himself outside the gates to the pet cemetery. The noise of the town celebration had faded behind him, and now the night was quiet and peaceful. Nosing open the gate, Sparky stepped inside. He walked past a sea horse's grave and then a statue of a Labrador. Then by a few house cats until finally he stopped—right in front of his own

grave. He couldn't read the words on the marker,
but he seemed to know that this was an important
place. It smelled . . . familiar. With a sigh, Sparky
lay down. Now all he could do was wait and hope
that Victor would find him and that he would be
allowed back home. . . .

Unaware that Sparky had escaped, Toshiaki had
come up with a project that would win the science
fair. The only problem was, he needed to steal
it from Victor. Which meant going to his house.
So he, Bob, Nassor, E, and Weird Girl from their
class had all met up in front of Victor's. Walking
up to the door, Toshiaki rang the bell.

"What are we going to say?" Bob whispered as
they waited.

Toshiaki rolled his eyes. Wasn't it obvious?
"We're going to ask him how he did the invisible
fish and his dog."

"What if won't tell us?" Bob asked.

Toshiaki's plan hadn't really gotten that far, but he didn't want to tell Bob that. Instead, he knocked on the door. It swung open with a squeak.

"Hello?" Toshiaki called out.

Suddenly Weird Girl's cat, who she had insisted they bring along, jumped out of her arms and raced inside. They all watched as Mr. Whiskers disappeared up the stairs. Toshiaki gave them all a look that clearly said, "Well, now we *have* to go in," and stepped inside. The others followed.

Since E was the only one of the group who had been to Victor's house before, they let him lead the way up the stairs to the attic. Once inside, they poked around, examining all Victor's odd gadgets.

"Cool," Bob said, observing the projector screens.

Toshiaki nodded absently. All the other experiments might be cool, but he was only interested in one—the bring-an-animal-back-to-life experiment. Scanning the room, he finally spotted the blackboard covered in doodles. But what caught his eye was the picture of Sparky in the center. This had to be it!

Leaning closer he, Nassor, and Weird Girl began to examine the formulas and theorems writing all over the blackboard. Some of it made sense to Toshiaki, but what he really understood was the pictures. In the biggest one, lightning hit a rod which sent electricity shooting down into Sparky.

A smile began to creep over Toshiaki's face. With the information they had gotten in the attic, he would be able to win the science fair— and maybe even become famous in the process. Tonight, they would bring the dead to life!

CHAPTER TWELVE

Back in New Holland's town square, everyone was blissfully unaware of the diabolical plot that several of their children were hatching. They were also blissfully unaware of the huge thunderstorm brewing overhead. Instead, they were watching as Elsa Van Helsing took the stage.

Nervously, she looked out over the crowd. Her uncle had talked her into, or rather forced her into, singing a Dutch anthem—in Dutch. He told her it was her duty as that year's Little Dutch Girl, but secretly she thought he just enjoyed torturing her every chance he could get. Taking a deep breath, she began to sing. The sooner she got through the song, the sooner she could get off the stage, go home, change back into normal clothes, and maybe find Victor and ask about Sparky.

As Elsa sang, Toshiaki and the others put their plan into action. They had gone their separate ways after leaving Victor's house, but they all had the same goal—bring an animal back to life.

So Toshiaki had gone to the pet cemetery and dug up Shelley, his pet turtle. Then he had carefully wrapped his "package," loaded it into a wagon, and headed home. He had set up some equipment behind the gardening shed in his backyard. As soon as he got home, he unwrapped the package and attached a kite to the animal's leg. But this was no usual kite string. Toshiaki had made it using extension cords. As he flew the kite higher and higher into the sky, he had to keep connecting new cords. But finally, the kite was high enough to be close to the growing storm clouds. Toshiaki leaned back and waited.

Nassor had also gone to the cemetery. He headed up the hill toward a gothic mausoleum. Approaching it with reverence for his pet lying at rest inside, he spoke: "Ah. The tomb of Colossus.

CHAPTER TWELVE

Soon you shall be awakened and we shall be reunited once again." Carefully, Nassor entered the tomb and clamped two clips attached to four Mylar balloons. He exited and waited to meet his beloved pet once again.

In the science room at the school, E was doing his own version of the experiment. He had found a dead rat in the garbage behind the school and pulled it out. It was definitely the victim of a run-in with a car, as evidenced by the track marks through its middle, but E figured it would work anyway. Placing the rat on the table, E grabbed the electrodes Mr. Rzykruski had used when he had made the frog's leg jump. Then he attached them to the rat. He didn't have a lightning rod but the electrodes should hopefully do the trick. He would have to wait and see.

Bob used his parent's pool to conduct his experiment. He had recycled his original science-fair project—the sea creatures. Ripping open the container, he dumped them all into the pool. Then he wrapped a wire around the long, metal pool skimmer. This would be his lightning rod. And the water would be the conductor. Bob wasn't much of a scientist, so now all he could do was wait and see if it would work.

Weird Girl, in typical Weird Girl fashion, had found the creepiest animal—a bat. Actually Mr. Whiskers had found it for her, but it didn't matter. A dead animal was a dead animal, right? So she pinned the bat to the corkboard in her room and used a butterfly wall hanging and a coat hanger to create a lightning rod. Sitting back, she and her cat looked out the window and waited for lightning to strike.

As Elsa continued to sing and Toshiaki and the others waited for their projects to come to life,

CHAPTER TWELVE

Victor frantically continued looking for Sparky. The thunderstorm that had been brewing all evening was coming to a head, and he didn't want Sparky to get caught out in the rain. But he had looked every-where. How could it be so hard to find one dog?

There was only one place left to look—the cemetery. As fingers of lightning cracked across the sky, Victor pushed open the gate and walked inside. Sweeping his flashlight back and forth, he cast long, scary shadows over the various gravestones. He aimed it at Sparky's grave, his heart pounding. Maybe he would be there, waiting for him. But the grave looked the same as it did before.

Walking over, he looked down at the grave and tried to think of something to say. Something that would make all of this better. That would make things go back to the way they used to be. But there was nothing he could say. Sighing, he turned, the beam of his flashlight sweeping across one of the larger tombstones . . . and a tail. Wait? A tail? Could it be? Victor aimed the flashlight right at the tombstone.

"Sparky!" he called out hopefully.

From around the edge of the tombstone, two big eyes peered out. Spotting Victor, Sparky let out a joyous bark and raced over. He jumped up, knocking Victor down. But Victor didn't care. He sat up, hugging his dog close to him.

"I thought I lost you," he said as Sparky wiggled and wagged his tail. "I don't ever want to lose you, okay? Promise you'll never go running off." Sparky gave him a lick.

For a moment, the boy and his dog just sat there, happy to have found each other. But then Victor noticed the two open graves and the shovels left next to them. That was a bit odd? Had someone else been there? Were they still there? And if they were, what on Earth were they doing?

CHAPTER TWELVE

* * *

The storm was getting stronger and stronger by the minute. In their various spots around town, Toshiaki, Nassor, Bob, E, and Weird Girl waited for the final part of their plan to take place. They didn't have to wait long.

As Toshiaki watched in amazed horror, his kite got swallowed up by the dark clouds. The extension cord kite "string" jerked and tugged. Then, as he stood there, the hair on his head began to rise. Toshiaki squatted down and covered his head, trying to make the hairs go down. But it didn't work. All he ended up doing was knocking over a bottle of Miracle-Gro which spilled on top of his pet. And then, just when Toshiaki thought things couldn't get worse, a bolt of lightning surged down from the sky, striking the cords and flowing right into the animal lying in the wheelbarrow . . .

Over at his house, Bob watched the pool and waited for something to happen. A lightning bolt crackled but hit the neighbor's backyard. Another bolt hit in the front yard. And then, finally, a bolt came tearing down, slamming right into the metal pool skimmer Bob had set up. The lightning traveled down the skimmer and then it crackled across the surface of the pool. When it was all over, a thin mist clung to the water's surface. . . .

In the cemetery Nassor's balloons were struck by lightning, causing them to burst. A surge of electricity traveled down the iron rod and right into the open grave. Nassor waited patiently outside the mausoleum. Had it worked?

At the school, lightning struck the building and surged through the power line and into the electrodes attached to E's rat. E jumped back, his heart racing. When the surge ended, he moved closer to take a look. The rat looked the same . . .

although it *was* looking a little less flat around the middle . . .

In her bedroom, Weird Girl was ready for her experiment to begin. She had pinned the bat to the corkboard, and the metal hangers were twisted into a rod. Now all she needed was the lightning. But when she turned to double-check on her bat, it was gone! Panicked, she looked around her room and saw Mr. Whiskers holding the bat in his mouth. Before she could get the bat away from Mr. Whiskers, lightning flashed down, striking the wire hangers. The girl ducked out of the way as it surged above her, heading for the hangers.

When the surge was over, she looked up. Mr. Whiskers looked okay. His fur was smoking a little and he appeared a little dazed, but otherwise he seemed fine. And then, as Weird Girl watched in horror, two giant bat wings unfurled from the cat's back. She gasped. Hearing the sound, Mr. Whiskers looked up and hissed, revealing two giant fangs. Then, with a flap of his wings, the newly created Vampire Cat flew out of the window into the stormy night. The girl gulped. What had she created? And more importantly, what had all the others created?

CHAPTER THIRTEEN

At that very moment, Toshiaki, Bob, Nassor, and E were discovering *exactly* what they had created.

After coming back to life, Sparky was still a regular dog—not counting a few stitches and neck bolts. But that was because he had been brought back out of love. What the others had done was due to jealousy, greed, and selfishness. Which meant the creatures they had made were bound to have some . . . deformities.

Inside the classroom, E swung a desk lamp over to take a closer look at his rat. On the upside, it had come back to life just as he hoped. On the downside, it wasn't a normal rat anymore. As E watched, the rat sat up. Then, with alarming dexterity, it began to unclip the electrodes attached to its body, as if it were human. It also seemed to have grown. Its legs were still little and mouselike, but it had a huge hump on its back and its snout was long and pointy. When it tilted its head back and howled, it sounded somewhere between a wolf and a mouse. The rat had become a were-rat! Gulping, E stepped back, hitting the desk lamp and casting a shadow of the Were-Rat on the wall. Then the rat reared up on its back feet, its teeth and claws extended, and began to make its way toward E. He was in big trouble. . . .

E wasn't the only one in over his head. Bob stood at the edge of the pool, staring into the water. The mist had cleared and left the water's surface smooth and clear. For a moment, Bob felt a rush of disappointment. The experiment hadn't worked.

And then, an almost-translucent hand reached up out of the water and grabbed the side of the pool.

As Bob watched, a sea creature pulled itself out of the water. But this was no ordinary sea creature.

The lightning had made it into something bigger—and scarier. It was skinny, with spindly arms and legs and large, webbed ears sticking out of its shrimplike head. Looking over at Bob, its wide eyes grew wider and it opened its mouth, revealing sharp, spiky teeth.

The Sea Monster wasn't alone. As it made its way out of the pool, dozens more followed. They were like an army of simian warriors. Some even carried bone tridents. And they all looked very, very angry.

Letting out a scream, Bob turned. "Victor!" he said aloud to himself as he ran away. "Victor will know what to do."

As Bob hightailed it out of his yard, Toshiaki was trying to figure out if his own experiment had worked. Standing there, he watched as the kite he had attached to his animal came crashing down, still smoldering. Looking over, he saw that the wagon was empty and next to it, the Miracle-Gro container lay on its side, also empty. Where had Shelley gone?

Suddenly, a massive turtle foot smashed down, crushing the wagon as if it were a toy. Toshiaki raised his head and gulped. Standing there was a giant turtle monster. It was bigger than a bus, and when it lifted its head to shriek at the sky, the sound was deafening.

Toshiaki fell backward and then began to scramble away as fast as he could. For a moment, he felt a rush of pride that he had brought back his pet turtle. But then the turtle let out another huge roar and the pride was replaced with utter terror. Turning toward the direction of downtown New Holland, the Turtle Monster saw the bright lights of the Ferris wheel. Distracted, it began to lumber off in that direction, leaving Toshiaki behind. As the turtle moved away, Toshiaki grabbed his bike and started riding in the other direction. He had to get help—fast!

Nassor was going to need help, too. In the cemetery, he watched as the earth around the grave began to rumble and shake as though something were trying to get out.

"Rise, Colossus," Nassor said. "Rise from your tomb!"

As he continued to urge his creature to rise, the ground shook even harder. A moment later a creature emerged from the ground. At first glance, it looked like a huge wad of tissues. But as it pulled itself up and out of the ground its shape became clearer. It wasn't tissues. It was a mummy hamster! Breaking clear of the ground, it stood up and extended its arms. The hamster took a few steps forward on its hind legs but then fell onto all fours. It began to lurch forward, dragging its hind leg. Nassor shuffled back as the creature continued to advance. a menacing look on its once cute and fluffy face . . .

Nassor had to find Victor. He would know what to do. He hoped. . . .

Victor was unaware that monsters had been unleashed upon New Holland. As the Mummy Hamster. Were-Rat. Vampire Cat, Turtle Monster, and Sea Monsters took to the streets. Victor was making his way home with Sparky.

"I'll get you charged up, boy," he told his dog. "You gotta be hungry."

Wrapped inside the blanket, Sparky wagged his tail. He *was* feeling a bit hungry and tired. All that running had taken a lot out of him. He wanted to go home and take a nice long nap on his bed in the attic.

But that wasn't going to happen.

Turning a corner. Victor did a double take.

Charging past was what looked like an army of . . .
giant shrimp? They were tall and skinny and oblivious to Victor as they marched along. Crouching
down behind a mailbox, he and Sparky watched
the creatures. They were chattering to each other
in some strange language, and occasionally one
would hit a mailbox with what appeared to be a
trident. Another purposefully trampled on a bed
of flowers. It was almost as if they enjoyed causing
destruction.

Suddenly, one of the creatures stopped. It was
the largest member of the army and appeared to
be its leader. It seemed to have noticed the lights
from Dutch Day in the distance. Giving an order
that sounded something like CHARGE, it opened
up a nearby manhole cover and disappeared into
the sewers. The army followed.

As soon as the coast was clear, Victor raced
home, Sparky at his heels. He needed to talk to

his parents. But when he got home, the door was wide open. "Mom? Dad?" he shouted. There was no answer. No one was home. They were probably still out looking for Sparky.

He was turning to go when Bob wheeled up the walkway on his bike. His face was red and he was panting from the effort of pedaling his bike.

"Victor!" he shouted. "I need your help!"

That wasn't what Victor wanted to hear. He had a sinking feeling he knew why Bob was here. "Did you see those things?" he asked. "They were like . . ."

"Sea Monsters," Bob finished.

"Really?" Victor said, raising his eyebrows. He could *sort of* see the resemblance. But weren't sea creatures supposed to be really small and live in water?

Bob nodded. Really. "You know how on the package, they're like in a happy kingdom and everyone's smiling? Well, they're not like that at all."

Before Bob could explain further, Toshiaki came racing up on *his* bike. The usually composed boy looked a mess. "Victor! I need your help!" he shouted from the sidewalk.

"I asked him first!" Bob shouted back.

"My problem's bigger!" Toshiaki screamed. He didn't have time for this. Turning, he pointed. In the distance, they could make out the giant turtle walking down the street, dwarfing the houses as he passed by them. It was like Godzilla had come to New Holland—in the shape of a turtle.

Sparky let out a bark and Bob shrugged. He had to admit, Toshiaki was right. His problem was definitely *bigger*.

Just then, the boys heard a scream coming from the direction opposite the Turtle Monster. Turning, they watched as their gym/science teacher raced past. And right behind her, running on its two back legs, was the biggest rat they had ever seen. Occasionally it would put one of its front feet down for a burst of speed. The teacher let out another scream and kept running.

The three boys exchanged looks. This was not good.

"I'll get my bike," Victor finally said, trying to sound braver than he felt. They had to get control of these creatures before they destroyed New Holland. The only question was, how were they going to do that?

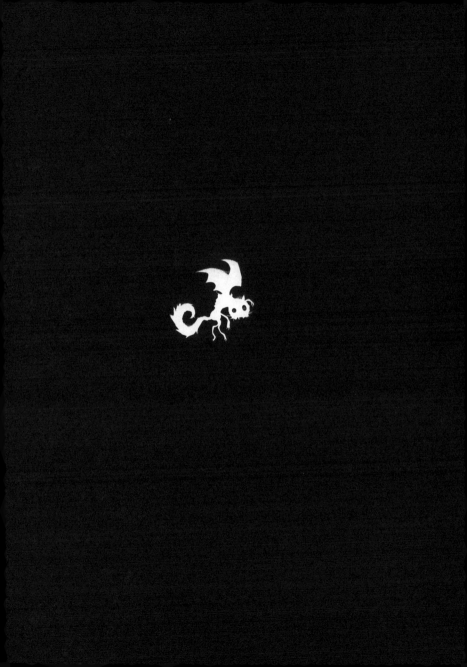

CHAPTER FOURTEEN

n the town square, the citizens of New Holland were unaware of what was coming their way. Backstage, Mayor Burgemeister was carefully snuffing out the candles on the crown Elsa had worn as part of her costume. While he was still reveling in the success of Dutch Day, Elsa couldn't wait for the day to be over.

"I told you there was nothing to worry about," the mayor said happily. "Safe as can be."

But he had spoken to soon.

"AHHHHHHHHHHHHHH!!!!!!!!" Out in the crowd someone let out a bloodcurdling scream. Then someone else screamed. Soon, everyone was screaming.

Poking his head through the curtain, Mr. Burgemeister scanned the crowd. What was all the fuss about? Then his eyes grew wide. Marching through town, crushing everything in its path, was the biggest, scariest-looking turtle the mayor had ever seen. Turning, he raced off, leaving Elsa behind to fend for herself.

The mayor ran as quickly as his short legs would let him, looking for a place to hide. As he ran, he saw the school's gym teacher fleeing a giant rat. His heart pounded even harder. Where were all these monsters coming from? Ducking inside a public bathroom, the mayor ran into a stall and slammed the door shut. Outside, he could hear shrieks as people ran away. He sat down and breathed a sigh of relief. He was safe in here.

Then he felt something poke him in the backside. With a squeak, he jumped up and turned around to look at the toilet. Coming out of the water was a Sea Monster carrying a trident. More were close behind and even more were coming out of the sink. Letting out his own scream, Mr. Burgemeister turned and ran.

* * *

Meanwhile, Victor's parents were hiding in a phone booth, hoping to stay out of sight. However, it wasn't long before the Sea Monsters were mischievously infiltrating the Frankensteins' refuge. Before the monsters could get to them, though, Victor's parents were saved by a giant turtle hand swooping down upon the phone booth. Mr. and Mrs. Frankenstein quickly scurried off to try and find Victor.

The Turtle Monster continued wreaking havoc as Nassor approached with Colossus, his pet hamster. The boy was drunk with power and commanded his pet to take down the giant and show him who was mightier. Nassor declared loudly, "Go Colossus! Kill! Kill!" As the Mummy Hamster prepared his fierce attack, the Turtle Monster stepped forward. His giant foot landed directly on top of Colossus, squashing him flat.

"Colossus?" Nassor asked sadly.

The angry turtle roared in Nassor's face in response and knocked Nassor back several feet, pushing him through a display and into a case—making him appear like a mummy himself.

Back in the center of town, the Turtle Monster had arrived. The air was filled with screams and shouts as people ran for their lives. After her uncle left her, Elsa grabbed Persephone and ran. She wanted to get home. Or find Victor. Or both. But seeing the giant turtle, Persephone began to squirm and shake at the end of her leash. Then she pulled so hard that she jerked free. Elsa watched, terrified, as Persephone disappeared into the stampeding crowd.

At that very moment, Victor, Toshiaki, and Bob arrived at the edge of the town square. Sparky was right behind them, panting a bit from the run, but ready to help in his own doggy way. They took in the screaming people, the marching Sea

Monsters, and the Were-Rat as it stumbled along.

Toshiaki climbed into one of the Ferris wheel carriages and started filming the chaos from high above the square. He laughed maniacally at the power of his creation. Suddenly, he heard a loud growl coming from behind him. It seemed the lights from the Ferris wheel had attracted the giant Turtle Monster. Toshiaki suddenly found himself face-to-face with his former pet! The giant turtle let out a monstrous roar, and Toshiaki started to panic. He tried to climb out of the carriage, but the Turtle Monster scooped him up by his pants and lifted him high into the air.

"No, no, no! Stop, you! Put me down!" Toshiaki cried. "I gave you life!"

Toshiaki dangled from the monster's powerful claw when suddenly the turtle stepped back and his massive tail smashed a nearby fuse box, sending sparks flying everywhere.

"Victor!" Toshiaki yelled. "I need your help!"

Victor saw a wire from the fuse box hissing and sparking near a puddle of water. That gave him an idea. He remembered from his science class that water conducts electricity. And the Turtle Monster just so happened to be standing in a huge puddle of water. As white sparks flew all around him, Victor ran over and grabbed the wire. Next, he threw it into the puddle directly under the Turtle Monster. Suddenly . . . ZZZZZZZ! A jolt of electricity shot up the turtle's leg. The Turtle Monster roared in pain, then crashed into a nearby tulip stall.

Now free from the Turtle Monster's deadly grip, Toshiaki quickly grabbed his video camera to continue recording the menacing scene—but it was too late.

As soon as Toshiaki put the camera to his eye, there was a huge explosion. Tiny pieces of turtle shell fell to his feet.

Toshiaki sighed. "Shelley . . ."

CHAPTER FIFTEEN

n town, it was now just Victor and Bob. The turtle had been the biggest of their problems, but the Sea Monsters were the most numerous. They had to get rid of them. More specifically, Victor wanted *Bob* to get rid of them.

"I think I read somewhere that salt could be deadly for these types of creatures," Victor said. But where could they get enough salt to take care of the army?

Glancing over, Victor spied the popcorn tent. He had an idea.

The Sea Monters had all gathered in one spot in the middle of the carnival. Yelling and waving his hands, Victor tried to get their attention. Finally, the Sea Monster king noticed Victor. Waving to his army, they began to march closer and closer to the boy. But this was just what Victor wanted. He ran into the popcorn tent and waited.

One by one the creatures came into the tent. Globbing together, they found themselves drawn to the warm, yummy smell of popcorn. As the Sea Monsters popped pieces into their mouths, they began to burst, creating a giant mess.

The Sea Monsters and the giant turtle were gone. But there were three monsters still on the loose. And Sparky had just found one of them. Spotting Persephone through the crowd, he barked, trying to get her attention. Then he noticed that she was facing off with the largest rat in the history of rats. The big, black creature had chased the gym teacher up the maypole, where she was hanging on for dear life. Persephone had raced over to help but was now caught in a face-off with the mutant rat.

Running over, Sparky and Persephone ganged up on the Were-Rat. They growled and inched closer, step by step. The rat hissed and snapped at them, trying to hold its ground. The dogs kept coming. Suddenly, the rat lunged, taking a bite out of Sparky's leg.

But Sparky wasn't a regular dog. He had electricity pumping through his veins. So the bite didn't hurt Sparky—but it *did* hurt the rat. A ZAP of electricity shot through the rat. As the dogs watched, the Were-Rat turned back into a regular rat. It took one look at the dogs—which were now much larger than it was—and scurried away.

Sparky looked at Persephone and wagged his tail. She wagged hers. Then they moved closer, their noses almost touching . . .

"Persephone!"

The sound of Elsa's voice surprised both dogs and they jumped back. Elsa was running toward them, happy to see her dog safe and sound.

But just as she was about to reach them, the

Vampire Cat swooped out of nowhere and scooped up Persephone.

"No!" Elsa screamed as the Vampire Cat flew away with Persephone. Sparky let out a bark as Elsa began to chase after her dog. Running as fast as his little legs could carry him, Sparky followed.

The Vampire Cat seemed to be heading right toward the windmill. Elsa quickened her pace and as she ran, she tore off the annoying blond wig. The synthetic hair kept getting in her eyes. Tossing it onto the ground, she kept running.

Sparky wasn't as fast as Elsa. He wanted to keep up with her and help Persephone, but his short legs wouldn't let him. He was going to need help. Seeing the wig, he grabbed it in his mouth and headed back toward town. If he could show Victor the wig, he could make him understand what was going on.

CHAPTER FIFTEEN

But back in town, things weren't going as planned. With all the lights out, the citizens of New Holland had grabbed torches to help them see. Those, combined with their Dutch Day outfits, made them look like a medieval mob out on a monster hunt. And they were almost as angry as a medieval mob.

Sparky didn't know any of that, though, when he raced up to Victor's parents. They were surrounded by other parents. Dropping the wig, he began to bark, trying to explain what had happened. He picked the wig up and shook it again, just like the bat had picked up Persephone. But all the humans saw was a dog that looked a little, well, beat-up, going crazy.

Having escaped the Sea Monsters, Mr. Burgemeister was trying to stop Dutch Day from being completely ruined. He heard the commotion and pushed his way through the crowd. Seeing

Sparky, his eyes grew wide. Then he saw Elsa's wig and grew furious. He took a menacing step toward Sparky. Sensing he was in trouble, the dog gave one last bark and then turned and ran back in the direction of the windmill.

Behind him, Mayor Burgemeister raised his torch high. "That dog is after Elsa!" he cried. "After him! Kill the monster!" Then, with the whole town following, he began to run after Sparky.

CHAPTER SIXTEEN

When Sparky arrived at the base of the windmill, he could hear Persephone barking inside. She sounded scared. With the angry mob just behind him, Sparky raced through the open door into the windmill.

Inside, he saw the Vampire Cat creeping toward Elsa and Persephone, pushing them both further up into the rafters of the windmill.

A mob led by Mayor Burgemeister had chased Sparky to the windmill. They had seen the dog dash inside.

"Quick!" Mayor Burgemeister shouted. "Before he gets out!" He began waving his torch, signaling the crowd to storm the building. But as he moved his torch back and forth, its flame inadvertently came into contact with one of the windmill's cloth sails. Instantly, the sail was engulfed in flames. The blades kept turning, fanning the flames.

Unaware of the fire. Elsa leaned out one of the windows. Seeing the people below. she cried out, "Help!"

"Elsa?!" Mayor Burgemeister exclaimed, confused. She didn't seem hurt. In fact, she seemed like she wanted them to help her with something—not save her.

Just then, Victor, Toshiaki, and Bob arrived on their bikes. Hopping off, Victor raced over to where his parents were standing. "Where's Sparky?" he asked.

His mother leaned down and put her hands on his shoulders. "He went inside," she said gently. "Victor, he's . . ."

Before she could finish her sentence, Victor shrugged her away and ran toward the windmill.

"Victor! Get back from there!" his dad shouted. The windmill was moving, shifting to one side as its base started to collapse due to the fire.

CHAPTER SIXTEEN

Victor soon reached the top, where the Vampire Cat had cornered Elsa and Persephone. The girl and her dog were out on the now-fully-ablaze sails of the windmill. Victor went to help them, but that only drew the attention of the Vampire Cat. The monster tried to attack young Victor—but Sparky launched through the windmill window and attacked the creature first. Sparky would not let Victor get hurt!

With the Vampire Cat distracted, Victor bravely inched his way out onto the sails to save Elsa and Persephone. Elsa lost her footing, but Victor quickly reached out to her. He just barely caught Elsa and the frightened poodle. Victor looked around and grabbed a nearby rope. He tied it around the two and lowered them to safety.

Victor turned his attention back to Sparky, who was still fighting off the fearsome Vampire Cat as they both clung to the sails of the burning windmill.

"Sparky!" Victor cried. Sparky jumped into Victor's arms, safely away from the Vampire Cat.

Undeterred, the Vampire Cat made one final lunge toward them—knocking Victor off the side. The large crowd below gasped in horror as Victor and the Vampire Cat plummeted through the floorboards and disappeared into the bowels of the windmill.

Mr. and Mrs. Frankenstein tried to run in after their son but the firefighters wouldn't let them through. "That's my son in there!" Victor's father protested.

Inside the windmill, Sparky battled the flames and raced to the bottom to find both the Vampire Cat and Victor unconscious on the floor. Grabbing Victor by the collar, Sparky used all the strength in his little body to drag Victor out of the windmill and to safety.

Victor's parents and the rest of the crowd

watched, waiting for some kind of life to emerge from the wreckage. . . . Suddenly, they burst into a cheerful roar! It was Victor and Sparky! They were safe! Sparky barked with joy. But just as Victor awoke, the Vampire Cat reared up from out of the flames and dragged Sparky back into the collapsing windmill!

The Vampire Cat knocked Sparky backward and cornered him against the wall. He bared his fangs and moved in for the kill.

Sparky steeled himself for the worst as a flaming shard of wood broke off the rafters above and plummeted to the ground. But at the last second, Sparky moved out of the way. The shard missed him—and drove right through the Vampire Cat, ending its rampage for good!

Sparky tried to run for the door when the windmill finally collapsed, to the horror of Victor and the crowd outside.

* * *

As the sun began to rise, Victor stared at the remains of the windmill. The fire was out, but all that was left of the town's landmark was rubble and ash.

Standing beside his parents and classmates, Victor wiped away a tear, leaving a smudge of ash on his cheek. Sparky was gone. After everything they had been through, he was really, truly gone. Victor sniffled. What was he going to do now?

"I found him!"

Victor's head snapped up. One of the firefighters was emerging from the debris, holding Sparky. The little dog was singed, and he looked more black than white, but he was in one piece.

The firefighter placed Sparky gently on the ground. Racing over, Victor kneeled down next to him. The dog wasn't breathing. Everyone started to huddle around, trying to see but Bob held up a hand. "Give him room," he said. Victor had done so much for the town, they owed him some respect.

Victor put a hand on Sparky's side. Well, at least now he could say good-bye. Again.

Kneeling down next to his son, Mr. Frankenstein looked at Sparky. "Is there anything we can do for him?" he asked.

Victor's head shot up. Wait? Did his dad mean what he thought he meant? "But you said . . ."

"Sometimes adults don't know what they're talking about," Mr. Frankenstein said.

Victor smiled. In that case, yes, there was something they could do. . . .

As the sun continued rising over New Holland, a dozen cars pulled into a circle around Sparky. Lifting the hoods of their vehicles, the various townsfolk attached one end of their jumper cables to the batteries. The other ends were attached to two main lines. Victor attached those to Sparky.

When everything was set up, Victor took a deep breath and nodded at his father. "Give it everything you got!" Mr. Frankenstein cried.

In unison, all the drivers revved their engines. As the cars roared, Victor connected one last cable.

As the electricity raced through the cable and into Sparky, his leg gave one violent twitch.

"Okay!" Victor cried out. He disconnected the power as his dad waved for everyone to cut their engines.

A hush fell over the circle as the citizens of New Holland waited. Sparky wasn't moving. Leaning over, Victor touched his dog gently. "It's okay, boy," he said, his voice barely a whisper. "You don't have to come back. You'll always be in my heart."

Victor continued to pet Sparky's head. He had

done everything he could. He would miss his dog so much but . . .

Thump, thump.

Victor looked back. Sparky's tail was wagging! Then, as he watched, Sparky opened one eye. Then the other. And then, he sat right up and started licking Victor!

As the crowd around them cheered and applauded, Victor pulled Sparky in for a big hug, happier than he had ever been. In the midst of the celebration, Persephone pushed through the crowd, her white-streaked hair glistening. She bounded up to Sparky, and in the joy of their reunion, they shared a sniff and a jolt. It seemed life was pretty good. . . .